Curious George

The Movie

Adapted by Jasmine Jones
Motion picture story by Ken Kaufman
Motion picture screenplay by Ken Kaufman and David Reynolds
Based on the books by Margret and H. A. Rey

Printed in the United States of America
WOZ 10 9 8 7 6 5 4 3 2 1
www.curiousgeorgemovie.com
www.curiousgeorge.com

Curious George®
The Movie

The Deluxe Movie Storybook

This is George. George was a good little monkey and always very curious.

George was looking for someone to play with. He wondered what would happen if he put a crocodile egg in a bird's nest. He wondered what would happen if the chameleon had to change too many colors. He wondered what would happen if he used pomegranate juice to paint the baby animals.

The same thing always happened: trouble!

One day, George saw a giant banana. He was more curious than ever. The giant banana was moving through the bushes! George decided to follow it.

When George peeked through the bushes, he saw that the banana wasn't really a banana. It was a yellow hat and a tall man was wearing it. But not for long . . .

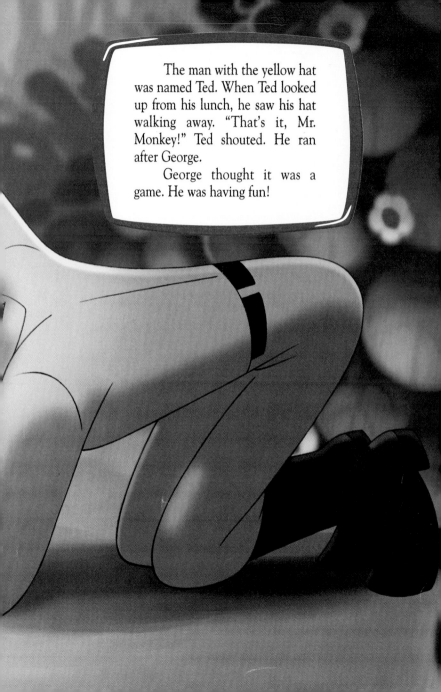

The man with the yellow hat was named Ted. When Ted looked up from his lunch, he saw his hat walking away. "That's it, Mr. Monkey!" Ted shouted. He ran after George.

George thought it was a game. He was having fun!

Finally, Ted decided to give the hat to George. "It's all yours," Ted said.

George couldn't believe it. No one had ever given him a present before.

Then Ted walked away. He was leaving the jungle. But George wanted to keep playing. He decided to tag along.

At the port, there was so much to see and do! But Ted could not stay and explore. He headed for a big ship that was about to sail to the United States. He had to go back to the museum where he worked.

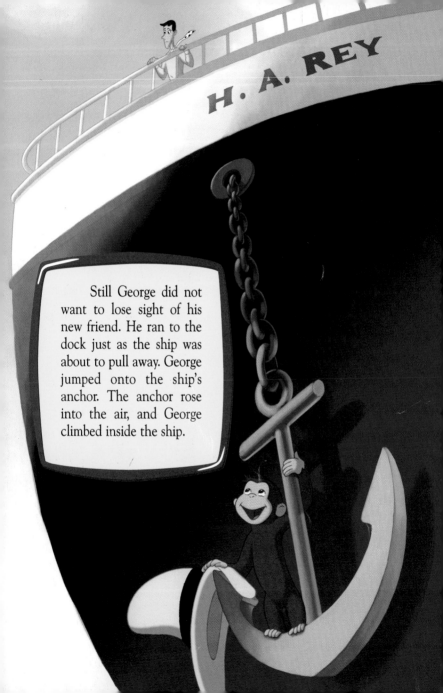

Still George did not want to lose sight of his new friend. He ran to the dock just as the ship was about to pull away. George jumped onto the ship's anchor. The anchor rose into the air, and George climbed inside the ship.

George found a large room inside the ship. This was the cargo hold, where all of the ship's food and supplies were stored.

There was a lot for a curious monkey to explore! When George pushed a button on a trunk, a pile of clothes popped out.

George also found crates full of fresh fruit. Yum!

The ship sailed across the ocean.
When it finally stopped, George got off and
looked around. He was in a giant city!

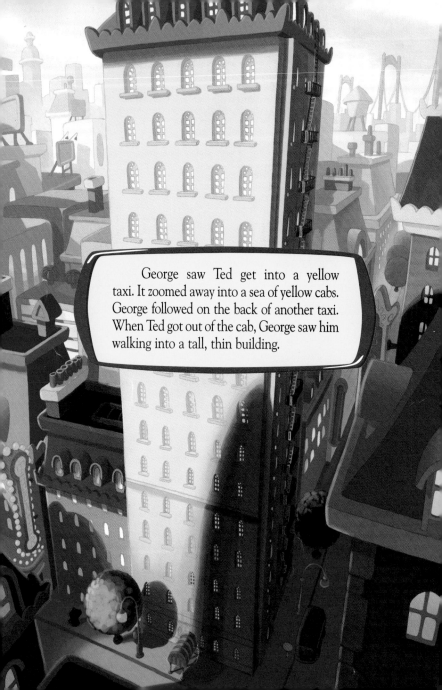

George saw Ted get into a yellow taxi. It zoomed away into a sea of yellow cabs. George followed on the back of another taxi. When Ted got out of the cab, George saw him walking into a tall, thin building.

George followed Ted right inside his apartment. Ted was surprised to see his yellow hat on the floor. He thought he had left it in Africa. When he picked up his hat, Ted discovered George underneath!

George was so happy to see his friend again. Unfortunately, Ted was not allowed to have pets in his apartment. When someone knocked on his door, Ted hid George in the bathroom. "Stay right in there," Ted told George.

But George was too curious. He went exploring.

Upstairs, George found an apartment that was being painted. He decided to help!

When Ted had to go to work, he knew that he couldn't leave such a curious monkey alone in his apartment. So Ted took George to the museum with him.

Ted left George in his office while he went to a meeting. George didn't mind. Ted's office was full of interesting things. Maybe the museum was full of even more interesting things? George was curious.

Soon George found . . .

. . . a dinosaur! But when George climbed up its bones, the dinosaur tipped over. Bones fell everywhere. The big mess meant big trouble for George and Ted.

That night Ted tried to go home. But the doorman wouldn't let him in.

"No pets," the doorman said.

So Ted took George to the park. They sat down under a tree. George saw some beautiful fireflies. But they didn't taste very good!

Then Ted and George admired the stars together. Ted told George some jokes and they both fell fast asleep.

The next morning, Ted took George to the zoo. George loved the colorful balloons. He collected a few.

The children at the zoo tried to guess George's name.

"Jojo?" one asked.

"Hercules? Bananas?"

"Call him George," Ted said.

The children gave George their balloons. Now George had a big bunch. When the wind blew, George sailed into the air!

"Mister!" shouted one of the kids. "Your monkey is floating away!"

George had never been so high up before.

"Don't be afraid!" Ted called. He saw a balloon man. Ted grabbed a big bunch of balloons from him and floated after George. "Wait for me!" Ted hollered. He snatched a kite on his way up to help him steer.

Finally, Ted caught George. They floated over the city together. What a view!

When they came down Ted took George back to the museum, but it looked like Ted had lost his job. They had nowhere to go. Ted decided that George should go back to his home in Africa.

"It's for the best, George," Ted said.

Two monkey-catchers came and caught George. They put him in a cage and then on a ship to Africa.

After spending an afternoon alone Ted decided that he missed George too much. "I'm off to save George!" Ted declared.

He knew that he had to hurry. The boat for Africa was leaving soon. Ted borrowed his friend's truck and raced off to the docks.

Ted reached the ship in time. He searched the cargo hold until he found George's cage. Ted broke the lock and gave George a huge hug.

George was very happy to see Ted again. There was only one problem. He and Ted were still on the ship—and it had started moving. They were on their way already!

In Africa, George helped Ted discover an amazing new exhibit for the museum. It would help Ted get his job back.

When they came home, everyone was glad to see them.

Where would George's curiosity take them next?